ANIMAL PARADE

Jakki Wood

Bradbury Press   New York

Maxwell Macmillan International
New York   Oxford   Singapore   Sydney

Aa   aardvark • antelopes • anteater • ants

Bb beaver • bison • bear • bee • butterflies

Cc camel • chimpanzee • caterpillar • crab •

coyote • cockatoo • crocodile • cheetah

Dd
dolphin • dromedary • duck • ducklings

Ee   elephants • emu

Ff

fly · flying fish · flamingos · frog · fox

Gg giraffes · grasshopper · gorilla

Hh

hippopotamus • hamster • hornbills

Ii   ibex • iguana • ibis • insects

Jj   jaguar • joey   Kk   kangaroo •

kittens • koalas • kookaburra • kiwis

Ll

lemur • lion • llama • lynx • lizard

Mm moose • monkeys • mice • macaw

Nn narwhal · numbat **Oo** owl ·

ostrich • octopus • orangutan • okapi

Pp

panda • pig • parrots

penguins • pelican • porcupine

Qq quetzals • quails • quokka • quoll

Rr   raccoon • rhinoceros • rat • reindeer

Ss   sea lion • shoebill • snails • skunk • snakes

Tt

tortoise • tiger • tapir

Uu umbrella bird • uakari   Vv vipers • vulture

Ww walrus • wombat • wolf • warthog

Xx ox • x-ray fish

Yy yapok • yak

Zz   zebra fish •   zorilla • zebra